The
Year
of the
Book

The Year of the Book

by ANDREA CHENG

illustrated by ABIGAIL HALPIN

Houghton Mifflin • Houghton Mifflin Harcourt • Boston New York 2012

Text copyright © 2012 by Andrea Cheng
Illustrations copyright © 2012 by Abigail Halpin

Houghton Mifflin is an imprint of
Houghton Mifflin Harcourt Publishing Company.

www.hmhbooks.com

The text of this book is set in Berkeley Oldstyle.
The illustrations are drawn with pen and ink and digitally colored.

Library of Congress Cataloging-in-Publication Data
Cheng, Andrea.
The year of the book / written by Andrea Cheng ; illustrated by Abigail Halpin.
p. cm.
Summary: Follows a young Chinese American girl, as she
navigates relationships with family, friends, and her fourth-grade
classroom, and finds a true best friend.
ISBN 978-0-547-68463-5
1. Chinese Americans—Juvenile fiction. [1. Chinese Americans—Fiction.
2. Best friends—Fiction. 3. Friendship—Fiction. 4. Schools—Fiction.]
I. Halpin, Abigail, ill. II. Title.
PZ7.C41943Ye 2012
[E]—dc23
2011036331

Manufactured in the United States
DOC 10 9 8 7 6 5 4 3 2
4500366489

My dad   Me,   My brother,   My mom
              Anna Wang   Ken

PRONUNCIATION GUIDE

Grandma - *Nai Nai (ni ni)* 奶 奶

Hello/How are you? - *Ni hao (nee how)* 你 好

Thank you - *Xie xie (shieh sheih)* 谢 谢

Sky - *Tian (tien)* 天

One - *Yi (ee)* 一

Two - *Er (are)* 二

Three - *San* 三

Four - *Si (seh)* 四

China - *Zhong guo (jung gwo)* 中国

Give it to me - *Gei wo (gay wo)* 给 我

Friend - *Peng you (pung you)* 朋友

Stuffed bun - *Bao zi (bao dze)* 包 子

I'm sorry - *Dui bu qi (doay boo chee)* 对不起

Happiness - *Xing fu (shing foo)* 兴 福

CONTENTS

1 School 1

2 Cleaning Day 10

3 Chinese School 21

4 Science 32

5 Halloween 41

6 Giving Thanks 54

7 Get Well Soon 62

8 Winter Break 72

9 Spending the Night 84

10 Saturday 93

11 Christmas 101

12 Icicles 107

13 Sewing 114

14 Absent 121

15 Staying Home 125

16 Persuasive Writing 133

17 Spring Break 138

One

School

Ray, the crossing guard, is waiting at the curb in his orange vest that catches the sunrise.

"How's my girl?" he asks.

I show him the lunch bag that I sewed yesterday.

"Well if that's not the prettiest lunch bag I've ever seen." He tests the drawstrings.

"It's fabric left over from my bedspread," I tell him.

"So your lunch matches your bed." Ray admires my handiwork.

Laura and Allison join us at the curb. "How many more minutes until the bell, Ray?" Allison asks.

Ray glances at his wristwatch. "You got about three minutes today, girls." Then he walks into the intersection and holds out his arms so we can cross.

I'd rather stay with Ray than go onto the fourth grade playground where Laura and Allison stand so close that there's no space left for me.

"Hey, what's that?" Laura asks, noticing my bag.

"A lunch bag," I say.

"Homemade?" Allison asks.

I nod.

She looks at Laura. Their eyes meet.

We start out with the word of the week. Ms. Simmons writes it on the board. Perseverance. Laura's hand shoots up before Ms. Simmons has even finished the last letter. She knows more words than the rest of us.

"It's when you don't give up," she says.

Ms. Simmons nods. "Can someone give us an example of perseverance?"

Lucy raises her hand. "Like when I learned to play basketball," she says.

Ms. Simmons tells us to write a paragraph about a time that we were perseverant. Laura starts right away. I don't know how she thinks of ideas so fast. I stare at the blank paper. Then I see my lunch bag that's on top of my books and that gives me an idea. On the top of my paper I write my name, Anna Wang, and the title, Making a Lunch Bag. I skip a line and then write:

Making a lunch bag is not as easy as it looks. First I cut the rectangles too small because I forgot about the seam. Then I cut them again and made them bigger but I sewed the casing backwards.

Allison glances at my paper. She leans over and says, "Perseverance has to be something that takes a really long time." She shows me her title: *Learning to Ride a Two-Wheeler.*

The blood rushes to my cheeks. Writing about making a lunch bag is stupid but it's too late to start over. I don't think Ms. Simmons will understand what

I'm talking about, especially if she doesn't know how to sew. I glance at the clock. Time is going by and I have only written a few sentences. I pick up my pen and write,

> When I finally thought that my lunch bag
> was done, I couldn't figure out how to get
> the drawstring threw the casing.

When I reread my sentence, I notice that I wrote "threw" wrong because it should be "through," but when I erase it, my paper is a mess.

Ms. Simmons asks if anyone wants to read their paragraph out loud. Allison raises her hand. "When I was in first grade, I got a two-wheeler for my birthday, but I couldn't ride it. Then my dad put on the training wheels and I could sort of ride but not very well." She reads in a monotone and I stop listening. I'm thinking about how I had to take all the casing stitches out of my bag and sew it down the other way. The second time, I made it too narrow for the drawstring. When Allison is done, four other people say they wrote about learning to ride a bike. I bet nobody wrote about sewing a lunch bag.

The whole time that Allison is reading, Laura is still working on her paragraph. She has covered the page and now she's writing on the back. She must have been very perseverant about something to write so much.

Ms. Simmons collects our papers, and then it's time for reading.

We can read whatever books we want. Laura and Allison take two different Princess Diary books off the shelf but I brought my own library book called *My Side of the Mountain*. Soon I am with Sam, hollowing out a stump to make my own little house. Sam likes to be by himself in the forest. He has a pet falcon named Frightful for company and to help him hunt for food.

When the bell rings, I'm startled because Sam is in the middle of catching a deer. He's going to cure the meat so he'll have food in winter and he'll use the fur for clothing. I feel sorry for the animal, but at least he's not wasting any part of it. I want to keep on reading but I have to close my book because Ms. Simmons says reading and walking at once will get you into trouble. She knows because she did it and ended up with a big knot on her forehead. We head outside for recess before lunch.

I stand by the fence. Laura and Allison and Lucy come my way. "My mom can type so fast you can't even see her fingers," Laura says. She moves her fingers like she's at a keyboard.

"Is she a secretary?" Allison asks.

Laura shakes her head, making her blond hair fly all over. "Executive assistant."

"My mom's a high school principal," Lucy says. "You should see the kids when my mom walks by." She nods down at us like she is the principal and we are the students. "It's all about respect."

I hunch my shoulders.

"Have you ever heard of Hammond High?" Lucy asks. "That's her school."

"Hey, Anna, what about your mom?" Allison asks.

I can't just say that my mom vacuums and mops every Saturday or that she learned English almost perfectly because she is very perseverant and now she is going to college so someday she can be a nurse. "She works in one of those high-rises," I say. "With a view of the river."

"In an office?" Lucy asks.

"Sort of."

Allison looks over my head at Lucy. Then she and Lucy and Laura link arms and walk toward the tetherball.

My brother, Ken, and the other third-graders are in the grassy area, chasing each other up and down the hill. Last year Laura and I were there too, and when we got sweaty, we sat in the shade of the school building and played a Chinese game with little rocks that Mom taught me, kind of like jacks without the ball. But this year Laura found Allison and Lucy. I found Ray but he goes home while we're at school.

The boys are kicking a soccer ball across the field. Tai is in front, moving the ball like lightning with his feet. I like Tai and I'm a fast runner, but I don't like playing soccer because I get mixed up about which side is my goal. Once I scored a point for the wrong team and everyone yelled at me.

I sit down on the blacktop and open my book. Sam skins the deer and hangs the hide so it can dry. Later he plans to sew himself deerskin pants and a shirt. I wonder if he'll remember that seams take up a lot of room. When I made my rectangles too small, I cut new ones out of more leftover material, but Sam doesn't have extra deerskin. Maybe he should try a pattern out of paper first the way Mom does when she sews. But he probably doesn't have paper to spare.

"Anna." Ms. Simmons is calling. "Hurry. It's time for lunch."

There is nobody left out on the playground except me. I go to the back of the line behind the boys who are always messing around.

❊ ❊ ❊

On the way home from school, Ray has five acorns for me. I put them in my empty lunch bag. "That bag comes in handy," he says. "I wish I had one."

"They're not hard to make."

"I'm not so sure about that." He shakes his head. "Now you have a nice afternoon, hear?"

Laura and Allison are way ahead of me. Ken is talking and laughing with his friends. I take out my book and read-walk all the way home.

Two

Cleaning Day

When I wake up Saturday morning, the house feels quiet. Dad is a manager at Quik Stop so he has to work lots of shifts, even on weekends. Ken spent the night at his friend Alan's house. Mom fills her bucket with cleaning supplies while I eat my cereal.

"Hurry, Anna," she says. "The bus won't wait for us, you know."

"I don't feel like going today," I say, chewing slower than usual.

Mom puts her lips together.

"Laura and Allison stay by themselves all the time," I say. "I mean, we're already in the fourth grade."

"Anna, go and get dressed."

"I'm not finished eating."

"You can have something else to eat at Mr. Shepherd's."

I take one more spoonful, push back my bowl, and amble into my room. I wish I had clothes like Allison's—sweater sets with two layers that match, and bras instead of undershirts. Yesterday in the school bathroom she showed Laura the silky straps with tiny adjustable buckles.

I pull on my jeans and the sweater Grandma Nai Nai knitted for me and sent from China. Mom is standing by the door, holding my jacket as if I am a first grader who has trouble getting her arms into the sleeves.

"I still don't feel like going," I say, taking the jacket and putting it on myself.

"Did you ever think about how Mr. Shepherd feels?" she asks. "Especially now that Mrs. Shepherd is gone?" Mom's voice is getting louder. "It's time you must think about other people." Then under her breath she says something in Chinese that I think means "selfish girl," or something like that.

I grab my book and we head out the door of our apartment.

It's only the beginning of October but already the weather is cold and rainy. I hold my book under my jacket as we walk to the bus stop. The whole world can see that Mom is carrying a bucket full of cleaning supplies. What if we run into Laura or Allison?

On the bus I sit by Mrs. Lukens and Mom sits right behind us. Mrs. Lukens works in the apartment building next to Mr. Shepherd's so we often run into her either on the way there or on the way home. "Something the matter today, Anna?" she asks.

I shake my head.

Mrs. Lukens smiles. "Here, take a piece of candy. And one for your brother, too."

"Thank you," I mumble, opening my book.

"It's a stage," she says, looking back at Mom.

"A stage?" Mom doesn't understand. There are some things she still doesn't understand in English.

"That means it will end soon."

"Good," Mom says, looking at me.

The window of the bus is dirty. People are hurrying on the sidewalk, bundled against the wind.

I read without stopping until we get off the bus.

Mr. Johnson, the apartment manager, steps out from behind the counter as soon as he sees us. "You grow about an inch a week, Anna," he says, patting my head.

"She is a weed," Mom says.

I look down. Mom should say *She grows like a weed*, not *She is a weed*. That's the kind of stuff she never seems to remember, no matter how many times I tell her.

"What's the matter?" he asks.

"Growing up pains," Mom answers.

Mr. Johnson nods. "I know about those. Only I call them growing old pains." He touches my chin. "Have a nice day."

I step into the elevator and open my book. Mrs. Watson gets in on the third floor. "Oh, Mary," she says to Mom. "I just can't thank you enough for putting away all my summer clothes the other day." She winces for a minute as she straightens out her back. "Since the surgery, I just haven't been the same."

"Nothing to thank," Mom says.

We get off on the fourteenth floor and ring Mr. Shepherd's doorbell. It usually takes him a while to get to the door in his wheelchair, but after a minute, he's still not there. Mom opens the door with her key. "That's strange," she says. "He usually tells me if he's not going to be here."

We hear Mr. Shepherd's muffled voice from the back door. "Mary, is that you?"

He is on the floor of the closet with his legs all folded funny.

Mom runs over to him. "Why didn't you call Mr. Johnson? He gave you the beeper, remember?"

Mr. Shepherd's face is covered with beads of sweat. His voice is thin. "I knew you and Anna would be here any minute." He stops to catch his breath. "And I don't really like to be seen sprawled on the floor like this."

I know what he means. Like I don't like to be seen on the bus with Mom and her bucket.

Mom holds Mr. Shepherd under one arm and I hold under the other. When he counts to three, we

pull up. Mr. Shepherd is a tall man, and for a minute I wonder if we can get him high enough, but he knows how to help. He reaches for the arms of his wheelchair, and finally he's back in the seat. I pick up his legs and put them on the footrests.

Mom gets a washcloth for Mr. Shepherd's forehead. "What were you looking for in the closet?" she asks, frowning.

"Thought I'd get some of Elsa's things in order," he says. He reaches for a dress hanging right in front. "Like this one right here, do you think it might fit you?"

"Maybe you should wait for your niece to come, help you sort everything," Mom says. "Did you say she is coming next week?"

Mr. Shepherd shakes his head. "You know there's nobody in the world Elsa would rather have wearing her favorite dress than you."

Mom blushes. "Thank you, Mr. Shepherd."

We get a few boxes from the storage area and start cleaning out the closet. Mr. Shepherd wants to give the books to Mr. Johnson since he likes mysteries. The shoes are for Mrs. Watson. The old letters fit neatly into a shoe box.

All that sorting tires Mr. Shepherd out. While he dozes in his chair, I sit on the floor and open my book. But for some reason, I don't feel like reading. I look out the big window in the dining room. The rain has finally let up and the sun is trying to shine. Far away you can see the bend in the Ohio River.

On the table is a pad of paper and I know Mr. Shepherd keeps colored pencils in a coffee can on his desk. I bring them to the window and sit down on the floor. I start with the hills in front, and then add the big buildings of the city in the middle. *To Mr. Shepherd,* I write on the bottom.

Mr. Shepherd opens his eyes. "You're quite the artist," he says, wheeling himself closer to me. "You know, Anna, Mrs. Shepherd just loved this view. That's the reason we took this

apartment, because of this window and this view. She never got tired of painting it."

"I didn't know she was an artist," I say.

Mr. Shepherd shakes his head. "Was she ever. Landscapes. That's what she liked. Rivers, mountains, ocean beaches. Next week when you come, I'll show you some of her paintings."

Mom puts the broom back in the closet and sets the mop out on the balcony to dry. Just before we leave, Mr. Shepherd tapes my picture to the front door. "Thanks. Thanks for everything," he says, waving from his wheelchair.

When we get onto the elevator, he is still watching us. He waves once more before the doors shut. Mom presses button number three. She looks at me as the elevator goes down. "You know, Anna, what I think? I think you are not so young anymore. If you want to stay home by yourself next time, that is fine."

The elevator doors open and there is Mr. Shepherd. "Knew I'd beat you," he says. "The other elevator's faster." He reaches into his pocket. "There's something

I thought you ought to have, Anna." He hands me a small metal box. I'm not sure if I'm supposed to open it right there in the elevator.

"Go ahead," he says, holding the elevator door open with his wheelchair.

Inside is a set of miniature watercolors and a tiny brush.

"She used to carry it wherever we went." Mr. Shepherd is holding tight to the armrests. "In case there was something that caught her eye."

"Are you sure you don't want—"

He opens his mouth, but his voice won't come out.

"Thank you," I whisper.

On the bus, Mom takes out her anatomy book to study for her test tomorrow. I open the watercolors and touch the small circles of red, blue, and yellow. Mrs. Shepherd used to give us seeds to plant. She made us her famous peach pies. But I never knew she was a painter.

"I'll come back with you next Saturday," I tell Mom. I'm not sure if she hears me or not. She is concentrating on a picture of the human body in her anatomy book and moving her lips to pronounce the words.

Three

Chinese School

$\mathcal{M}$om is learning how to drive so she is in the driver's seat and Dad sits next to her. "Speed up," he says. "You don't want all the other cars to pass you."

"It's okay. They can pass," Mom says, trying to move the car over. It feels like we're about to hit the curb.

"Be careful," Dad says, as Mom swerves around a pothole.

Mom already failed the driver's test once. She said the tester was unfriendly. He even kicked the door closed with his foot. Dad said she should have complained, but Mom said that if the supervisor got mad, she'd never be able to pass the test. "I'll keep practicing," she said. "Then there will be no way I can fail."

Mom hits the brake too hard at the red light and the car jerks.

"You should look farther ahead," Dad says.

I am starting to feel carsick. Finally we turn in to the driveway of the church that lets us use the basement for Chinese school. Me and Ken and Mom get out, and Dad slides over into the driver's seat.

A group of kids is playing tag. Auntie Linda sees us. *"Ni hao,"* she says, coming over and patting me and Ken on our heads. She's not really our aunt. We call all my mom's friends aunties. Auntie Linda says something about how beautiful Mom's dress is. It's the one from Mr. Shepherd, Mom explains. I know because I hear her say his name in English. Auntie Susan joins the conversation. After that I can't understand what they are talking about. I wish I could because they are nodding and listening so hard to Mom's story. She lifts her leg and her arms. Auntie Linda and Auntie Susan look at me and smile. Mom must be telling them how Mr. Shepherd fell down and we hoisted him back into his wheelchair.

"Hey, Ken," a boy named Ryan says, tapping Ken on

the shoulder. They go over and join two other boys. A group of girls is talking by the door. Auntie Linda says, "Anna, see the girl in the green skirt? That is my daughter, Camille."

I nod.

"Camille," Auntie Linda shouts. Then she says something to her daughter in Chinese. Camille looks at me and waves. Her face looks friendly, but I don't know her so I'm afraid to go over to the group. Instead I open my book and read standing up.

A bell rings and we all go into one big room.

Teacher Zhen puts a Chinese character on the board.

天

She starts talking about it in Chinese, and I have no idea what she's saying. The other kids are taking out their notebooks and copying down the character. They already speak Chinese, so now they are learning to read and write. But I can only say a few things like *ni hao* for hello and *xie xie* for thank you. Dad always tells Mom to speak to us in Chinese, but she doesn't because we don't know what she's talking about.

I take out my notebook and write Anna Wang on the top. Then I copy the character off the board. Two lines across and two down, one long and one short. *Tian.* The teacher points to the character and counts to four: *yi, er, san, si.* She is counting the lines. But what good is it to learn how to make a character if you have no idea what it means? "What's it mean?" I whisper to the girl next to me.

"Shhh," she says.

I'm almost done with *My Side of the Mountain* but I don't like this last part. Sam's family is going to find him and he'll have to go back and lead a normal boring life. I try to think of another way that the story could go. He could never be found and just keep on living in the woods by himself, but that's unrealistic. His family would keep looking for him until they found him.

Or he could be attacked by a bear or he could freeze to death, but those are endings that don't usually happen in kid's books. Adult books are probably different because they don't worry about terrible endings.

"*Gei wo.*" The teacher is standing over me. Her voice is loud and I have no idea what she is saying. She has her hand out but I don't know what she wants. The girl next to me points to my book. "Give it to her," she whispers.

"My book?"

She nods.

But it's a library book, and if I don't return it on time, we'll have to pay a fine and Mom will be mad. Plus, even though I can predict the ending, I still want to read it.

Teacher Zhen is waiting. I close the book and hand it to her.

Next we listen to a rap song in Chinese. Some of the kids already know it and say the words with the rapper. I like the way it sounds but I don't know what it's about.

I stare at the cracks on the wall. One looks like the map of a river with a thick part in the middle and smaller tributaries branching out. Another looks like the profile of a person's face with a big nose sticking out. Laura and her brothers have upturned noses like that, but my nose is small and flat. Once a boy in my class called me a Chinese flat face and I called him a big-nosed moose.

At eleven thirty a bell rings again and Chinese class is finally over. Camille stands next to me. "I didn't understand that song—did you?" she asks.

I shake my head. "I don't speak Chinese."

"I speak some, but that song is too fast."

"I don't speak any," I say. "Neither does my dad."

"ABC?" she asks.

"What?"

"American-born Chinese?"

I nod.

Mom has been talking to her friends the whole time. Her face looks happy and young. She never looks that way when she comes to pick me up at regular school because she is worried that maybe she won't understand every little thing. But at Chinese school she has so many friends.

Ryan asks Ken if he can come over for the afternoon. Mom knows his mom. She says that would be fine. Nobody asks me if I can go anywhere.

"Teacher Zhen took my book," I say.

Mom pulls her eyebrows together. "Why is that?"

I shrug. "I don't know what she's talking about anyway."

"How can you learn Chinese if you don't listen?"

Mom goes into the classroom to talk to the teacher. They keep looking over at me. I bet Teacher Zhen is telling Mom that I am a naughty girl who doesn't pay attention.

When Mom comes back, she hands me my book. "Teacher Zhen is very kind to give you another chance."

"I don't want another chance," I say. "I don't want to go to Chinese school anymore."

"Then what will you do when we go to China?" she asks.

"Dad manages and he doesn't know Chinese."

"And that is very difficult for him. A Chinese face but no Chinese words is not easy."

"He could learn if he wanted."

Mom shakes her head. "A language is hard to learn when you are old, but when you are young, it is easy."

"Then why didn't you teach us?" I ask. "You could have been perseverant."

Mom looks around, hoping that none of her friends hears the way I am talking to my mother. She steps away from me like I am not her daughter.

Dad pulls up to the curb and scoots over so Mom can sit in the driver's seat. She waits until all the other cars are gone before she pulls out of the parking lot.

"Speed up a little," Dad says once we are on the road. "If you go under the speed limit, the other drivers get irritated."

Mom pushes on the gas pedal and the car lurches forward, making my stomach turn.

Mom doesn't say anything to me during lunch. She doesn't ask me if I want more noodles or milk to drink. After we are done eating, Dad goes to work and Mom makes herself flashcards for every single bone in the human body with the word on one side and the definition on the other. She has to have them all memorized before the test. I know that when she was a girl, she had to memorize Chinese characters every day, so she is used to making flashcards.

The phone rings. It's Laura asking if I can come over. I bet she called Allison and Lucy first, and then when they couldn't play, she asked me.

"I can't," I say. "I'm busy now."

"What are you doing?"

I have to think of something fast. "Studying my Chinese," I say. "I have a lot of characters to memorize."

"Characters?"

"They're like words."

"So you can't come?'

"No."

"Call me when you're done."

"Okay," I say, even though I know I won't.

When I hang up, I take some file cards and start copying characters out of the Chinese book.

"You were not friendly to Laura on the phone," Mom says.

"She's not friendly to me either," I say.

"You shouldn't lie," Mom says.

"I didn't. I am practicing my characters."

"I thought you don't want to learn Chinese."

"I changed my mind," I mumble.

"You have to do the strokes in the right order," Mom says, showing me on one of her flashcards.

"I think it looks okay," I say.

"You think you know everything." Then Mom mumbles something in Chinese.

"What does that mean?" I ask.

"Impossible to translate," Mom says, turning back to her anatomy book.

Suddenly I really want to know Chinese.

I take the file cards and the Chinese book into my room. Mom is right. I wasn't friendly to Laura. But Mom doesn't see her at school, following Allison around like a puppy.

The phone rings and I hear Mom speaking Chinese so it must be Auntie Linda or Auntie Susan. She says my name and I know she is telling her friend what a terrible daughter I am. Tears come to my eyes.

I sit at my desk and look out the window. The leaves of the gingko tree across the street have turned yellow. I could write Mom a note and tell her I'm sorry, but I don't know what exactly I am sorry for. Instead I draw a picture of the gingko tree with the Jacksons' house behind it. I get a cup of water from the bathroom and use the small paintbrush to fill in my pencil lines with paint.

Next to the metal watercolor tin is the Chinese book. I wonder if the glossary has the word for "sorry." I look through the alphabet until I get to the s's. There it is: sorry, *dui bu qi*, followed by three characters.

对不起

I don't know what order to make the strokes in, but I copy the characters as well as I can onto the bottom of the paper. Then I go

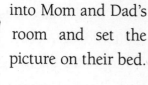

into Mom and Dad's room and set the picture on their bed.

Four

Science

On my way to school in the morning, there is a huge rainbow arching across the sky. I've seen little rainbows after it rains, but never one like this. And then I see that it is actually double. The second arch is faint but you can still see the colors. I hurry down the hill ahead of Ken.

"I've seen plenty of rainbows in my life," Ray says, "but I'd say this one is the most magnificent."

"It's double," I say.

Ray takes off his glasses. "You're right, Anna," he says. "I wonder what makes that happen." He smiles. "Could it be double raindrops?"

I know that water breaks the light into colors, but I

have no idea why. We watch until the rainbow fades. "How many more minutes, Ray?" I ask.

He looks at his watch. "You got about eight minutes today."

I see Allison coming down the hill. She has on a short skirt with a jacket that's made out of the same material. When she gets to the curb Ray asks her if she saw the rainbow.

Allison shakes her head. "Nope," she says. Then she sees Lucy. "I like your sweater."

"I like your jacket," Lucy says.

Ray looks at me. "Too bad you can't keep a rainbow in your lunch bag," he says, moving into the intersection so we can cross.

Too bad I can't stay with you instead of going to school, I want to say. Too bad we can't go to the library and find out what causes rainbows—single, double, or triple.

Ken joins his friends on the field. I walk over to the fourth grade girls. Laura is jumping rope and counting in Spanish. "I can count in French and German," Ashley says.

"I can say hello, like *bonjour*," Lucy says. She curtsies and nods her head like a French schoolgirl. Then she giggles. "Do you know what *Je t'aime* means?"

We shake our heads.

"I don't know if I should tell you." She looks around. "It means 'I love you.'"

The way Lucy talks makes me blush. "Hey, Anna, can you speak Japanese?" Allison asks.

"Chinese," I say.

"I mean Chinese?"

"A little," I say.

"Say something."

I think fast. "*Xie xie* means 'thank you,'" I say.

Allison tries to say *xie xie*, but it comes out sounding like *shee shee* instead of *shieh shieh*. She turns to Lucy. "Shee shee for letting me borrow your yellow sweater."

"How do you say 'you're welcome'?" Lucy asks.

I have no idea. "They don't say 'you're welcome' in Chinese," I say.

"Weird," Lucy says.

Soon lots of girls are saying *shee shee* for this and for that. What they don't know is that in Chinese, *shee shee* means you have to pee.

Laura drops the jump rope. "Did I tell you that I'm taking Irish dance classes?" Then she shows us the new dance she's learning, where you put your hand on your hip and spin around with a partner, who is Allison.

Finally the bell rings.

We go to Mr. Schmitz's room for science. There is a bathtub full of pillows in the back of the room where you can read when you're done with your work, but first we have to gather data. The data is observations about different bird nests that are out on the shelf. We have to write our observations in the columns on the worksheet.

"I bet this one is a blue jay's nest," Laura says. "And this one is a cardinal's."

Allison nods.

"This one is for a sparrow," Tony says.

How do they all know stuff like that? I have no idea what kind of bird makes what kind of nest. Anyway, those are not observations. Those are conclusions and Mr. Schmitz didn't say to conclude anything. *Observe* means to look closely, Mr. Schmitz says.

I see a pill bug on nest A, so I write that. And there is a small blue piece of paper stuck in the nest that might be from a candy wrapper. Nest B is falling apart on one side. As soon as I finish writing in the columns, I can turn in my paper and read in the bathtub.

I bend over to smell the nests. They all smell the same, like mud and grass. I write that across all the columns because there's no reason to write it over again five times.

"What are you doing?" Allison asks when she sees my big printing.

"They all smell the same," I say.

"Weird," she says.

I don't know if she means the smell or the writing or me.

My worksheet is getting messy because I'm in a hurry. I want to throw my paper away and start over

with a fresh one, but then I'll never have time to read in the bathtub.

Laura is drawing little pictures in each column. Everything is labeled very neatly. Allison's columns are full, too. She sees me looking at her paper and covers it with her arm.

I don't want to copy and I've done enough observing. Mr. Schmitz has some picture books that I remember from when I was little, like about Alexander's terrible day, so I get into the bathtub and read that one. Then I pick up a thick book with a picture on the cover of a girl who looks about twelve and a boy who looks about ten. I read the jacket. The kids are stuck

in a museum overnight. It sounds good so I lie down in the bathtub and open the book. I like the way it starts. The older sister is annoyed at her brother but you can tell she really likes him.

"Spacey Anna," Lucy says.

"Book girl," somebody whispers.

Everyone is looking at me. They are lined up by the door, ready to go. I climb out of the bathtub but my foot gets stuck on one of the pillows and I fall forward. Luckily I put my hands down so I don't really hurt myself, but my feet are tangled and the books are all over the place. Somehow I get up and make myway to Ms.

Simmons's classroom. Then I realize I still have Mr. Schmitz's book and I forgot to ask him if I could borrow it. I'll go back later to ask, but for now I have the book to read. These two kids find all this money in a fountain in the museum, and they start filling their pockets with it. That's not really stealing because the people left it there, but it sort of is because they didn't mean for it to go to these two kids.

"Are you all right?" someone asks.

I look up. Laura has her head next to mine. I don't know what she's talking about because I am in my book world. "What?"

"Did you hurt yourself when you fell?"

I shake my head. "I'm fine." Then I turn right back to my book. But I'm not in my book world anymore.

"Is that a good book?" Laura whispers.

"Yup."

"What's it about?"

"A girl and her brother who get shut inside a museum."

"Do they sleep there?"

I nod.

"I wish I could sleep in the museum. I bet it's peaceful there and I wouldn't have to listen to my dad shouting and breaking stuff."

"What stuff?" I ask.

Ms. Simmons is looking at us so we have to stop whispering. I wonder if Laura means he breaks cups and plates. Why would somebody break their own stuff, anyway?

Five

Halloween

Ken says I can be an astronaut with him. "You can wear the bigger helmet," he offers.

"I don't want to be an astronaut."

"So what do you want to be?"

"Nothing. I'm too old for that."

"You don't want to be anything?"

I shrug.

"Then you can't trick-or-treat."

"So?"

"Then we'll only get half as much candy,"

I like Kit Kats and Milky Ways. Ken likes bubble-gum, Tootsie Rolls, and Jolly Ranchers. We usually dump all our candy on the floor and sort it into piles and save the plain M&M's for Mom and the peanut ones for Dad. But it's not worth being an astronaut for that.

"How about vampires?" Ken suggests.

I shake my head. "I might not even trick-or-treat."

The doorbell rings. Michael wants Ken to come o and play, and when they come back in, Ken has fo a new Halloween partner.

It doesn't matter because Halloween is a dumb h day. Mom says in China they don't even have Hall een, so if we lived in China, we wouldn't have to w ry about costumes and everything. But why are th having a Halloween party at Chinese school then?

"It's funny," Mom says. "Nothing serious."

"You mean it's *for fun*, not *it's funny*," I say.

Mom frowns.

"Do I have to go?"

Mom hands me a bag of those Jell-O cups from the Asian market to give everyone.

"I hate these things," I say.

"Chinese children like them," Mom says, pulling her lips into a straight line.

✳ ✳ ✳

Teacher Zhen writes Halloween words on the board, like *witch* and *pumpkin* and *black cat*. I raise my hand.

南瓜   黑猫   巫婆

Witch   Pumpkin   Black cat

"Why are we learning these words," I ask, "when they don't even celebrate Halloween in China?"

"Talk Chinese in Chinese school," she says. She adds *haunted house* to our list of new words. I bet she made up all these Chinese Halloween words herself.

Everyone is supposed to say what they're going to be for Halloween, and Teacher Zhen tells us the Chinese word. One girl is going to be a princess. A boy says he's going to be Superman, which is the same in English and in Chinese. When it's my turn everyone is waiting.

"We don't celebrate Halloween," I say. "Chinese people aren't supposed to."

Everyone is looking at me. They can hardly believe it. Teacher Zhen goes on to the next kid who is going to be Harry Potter. When all the kids have had a turn to talk, we put the snacks in the middle of the table. The Jell-O cups are gone right away.

In the afternoon, Mom helps Ken and Michael with their astronaut costumes. They are going to use swimming snorkels for the oxygen thing and long underwear for the wet suits. It's very hot in their costume but they don't care.

"Did you change your mind, Anna?" Mom asks. "Laura's mom called to ask if you want to be Snap, Crackle, and Pop! with Laura and Allison."

I shake my head. "They can be Snap and Crackle or Crackle and Pop or Snap and Pop. Or they can ask Lucy."

Mom sighs. "You know, Anna, you could give things a chance."

"I do," I say. "All the time."

Mom looks at me like she's about to say something, but then she closes her mouth.

Mom has made caramel apples. That's what you're supposed to have for Halloween, caramel apples and apple cider and jack-o'-lanterns. I don't know why Mom does all these Halloween things when she never even heard of Halloween until she came to America. She followed a recipe in a cookbook called *Holiday Treats*.

Trick or treat is not until six o'clock and it's only five. Ken is running around the house chasing Michael in their astronaut suits, driving me crazy. I go upstairs to my room and open the window as wide as it goes. Outside it's warm but windy, as if the weather really might change. Sometimes on Halloween it's snowy and freezing but this year it feels almost like summer. There is a full moon rising behind our neighbor's house. I bet Ray is on his front porch, watching the full moon, too. If I knew where he lived, I could visit him for Halloween. Or Ms. Simmons. I know she lives in an apartment downtown, but I don't know exactly where.

I get the watercolors out of my desk drawer and paint a picture of the full moon. Some people say there's a man in the moon. Mom says in China they say it's an old lady. To me it looks like a frog, so that's what I paint.

The doorbell rings and I wonder why the trick-or-treaters are coming early. But it's Laura. She's not wearing a costume and her face is all red.

"What about Snap, Crackle, and Pop!?" I ask.

She doesn't answer.

"Come in," Mom says to her.

She steps inside the front door and takes a deep breath. "Smells good."

Mom offers her a caramel apple. She takes it and starts licking the caramel off the outside. I know she won't even eat the apple because she throws food out all the time at school. Mom says people all over the world are hungry so we save all our leftovers and eat them later.

Ken and Michael are decorating their candy bags. "Astronauts?" Laura asks.

"Yup."

"Aren't you trick-or-treating?" she asks me.

It's almost dark. Across the street I see the Wilsons' jack-o'-lantern glowing on their porch. "I don't know," I say. "I thought you were going to be Snap, Crackle, and Pop! with Allison."

"I'm not anymore."

"Why not?"

Laura's eyes get watery. Then she shrugs. "What do you want to be?"

"Little Blue and Little Yellow," I say quickly. As soon as the words are out of my mouth I wish I could take them back. *Little Blue and Little Yellow* is a book we had in preschool.

"I love that book," Laura says.

We tear big circles out of blue and yellow construction paper. Then we cover some cardboard with white paper and tape the circles onto it with packaging tape.

"How are we going to wear this costume?" Laura asks.

"I'll show you," I say, using the tip of the scissors to make two holes near the top of the cardboard. Then I put a piece of clothesline through the holes and knot it in front and in back so we can put the cardboard over our heads and it will hang on our shoulders.

"You're good at making things," Laura says, trying on the costume.

We go upstairs and look at ourselves in the bathroom mirror. Suddenly Laura hugs me. "Now we should turn green," she says.

"That used to be my favorite part of the book."

"Mine too," Laura says.

I look at the clock in the hallway and something catches my eye. Mom has put the landscape I painted in a thin black frame and it is hanging next to the clock.

"Fifteen more minutes until trick or treat starts," I say.

"What should we do while we're waiting?" Laura asks.

We go into my room. It's hard to move with the cardboard costumes on but there's no reason to take them off for fifteen minutes. Laura sees the watercolors on my desk. "Hey, where'd you get these tiny paints?"

"From a man whose wife used to be a painter," I say. "But she died, so he gave me them to me."

"I love miniature stuff like that," she says. Then she sees my moon picture. "Cool. I like how you made a design in the moon."

"It's a frog," I say.

"Why'd you put a frog in the moon?" she asks.

"That's what they think it is, in China."

Laura looks out the window. "What else do Chinese people think?"

Suddenly I feel so hot I can hardly stand it. How should I know what Chinese people think when I've only been to China once when I was a baby? I see two girls coming up the street wearing ice skating costumes. One of them is Allison.

I turn to Laura. "Why aren't you trick-or-treating with Allison?"

"She got mad at me," Laura says. "She's always mad if I don't do exactly what she says. So she decided to trick-or-treat only with Lucy."

I feel sorry for Laura. But then I know, if Allison hadn't changed her mind, I would be alone.

"It's six o'clock," Ken shouts up the stairs. "Come on."

Most of the houses we go to think we are a Visa card. They never even heard of Little Blue and Little Yellow.

But that's okay, because our bags are full of candy by the time we make it around the whole block.

When we get back home, Laura's mom comes to get

her. She helps Laura take the costume off and sets it on the floor. "Thank you," she says, more to Mom than to me. "You helped us in a pinch."

"A pinch?" Mom asks.

"You know how girls are," Laura's mom says, rolling her eyes.

Laura asks her mom if she can stay at our house for a while longer, but her mom says it's not nice to wear out your welcome.

"See you tomorrow," Laura says to me.

"Do you want to keep the costume?" I ask.

Laura shakes her head. "No thanks." She is already out the door.

Ken and I are sorting our candy on the rug. Kit Kats, M&M's, Jolly Ranchers, and bubblegum. "Where should I put this?" Ken asks, holding up some sort of sour apple candy.

"We need a miscellaneous pile."

"What's that mean?"

"Things that don't fit into other categories."

"Like odds and ends?" Mom asks.

I didn't even know she was listening while she was reading her anatomy book. "Sort of."

Mom writes the word on a file card. Then she asks me what "in a pinch" means.

"Like in trouble," I say.

"Like Mr. Shepherd was in a pinch when he fell," Mom says. Then she wraps two caramel apples in wax paper and puts them into a paper bag.

"Are those for Mr. Shepherd?"

Mom nods.

"Can we take them over now?"

Mom looks surprised. "We could wait until Saturday."

"But the apples will be old by then," I say. "And I bet Mr. Shepherd would like to see our Halloween costumes."

"I already took mine off," Ken says, "and I don't feel like putting that snorkel thing back on."

I pick up the yellow cardboard and put it over Ken's head. "Now you can be Little Yellow," I say. Before we leave, I run upstairs to get my moon picture.

✳ ✳ ✳

Dad waits for us in the car.

Mr. Shepherd opens the door right away. "Trick or treat!" Ken and I say at the same time.

Mom hands him the package. He opens the bag and takes a sniff. "Could it be my favorite caramel apples?"

Mom smiles. "Happy Halloween."

I hand him my picture.

"Thank you kindly," he says. Then he notices our costumes. "Now, let me guess. Something blue and yellow. What's that book? I used to read it to my grandsons."

"*Little Blue and Little Yellow!*" I say.

When we get back to the car, I look up at the tall building. The light is on in Mr. Shepherd's apartment. He is out on the balcony, waving, and in his other hand, he is holding my picture.

Six

Giving Thanks

It's almost Thanksgiving, so Ms. Simmons asks what we are thankful for.

"God," Lucy says.

William raises his hand. "I'm thankful because my grandmother almost died last year, but now she's doing better."

"I'm thankful for my whole family," Allison says.

Ms. Simmons tells us to write a paragraph about what we are thankful for in our lives. She says it can be something small or something big. She asks us to start with prewriting by making a list about all the possible subjects. Then we're supposed to pick one for the paragraph.

I don't know what to write. I am thankful that we have a library close to our house, but there's not much more to say about that. I am thankful that we have a big trunk full of fabric scraps. I am thankful that Ray is our crossing guard. But I don't think I can write a whole paragraph about any of those things. Time is going by and everyone around me has already decided what to write about. Suddenly I remember that on my last birthday, Dad brought home a big package with twelve mini cereal boxes from the Quik Stop. I could hardly believe it because we usually got the store brand cereal in big plastic bags because it was cheaper.

I start writing:

I am thankful because for my birthday, I got an unusual present from my dad. Twelve mini cereal boxes! We had so much fun deciding who would get which cereal. Finally I started with Frosted Flakes and my brother started with Corn Pops. That present lasted for a long time, and I saved the boxes. I still have them in a bag under my bed. I don't know what I'm going to do with them yet, but I'll think of something eventually.

"Finish up," Ms. Simmons says after a while. "And then I'd like you to do an illustration to go with your paragraph."

I draw twelve small boxes and on each one, I write the type of cereal that's inside: Corn Pops, Frosted Flakes, Froot Loops, Special K. That's the one none of us wanted.

Laura is drawing a picture of her family. She draws her mother in the middle, with her and her two brothers. Her father is on the edge of the page. She's good at drawing the faces with real expressions. Her father has a mad face with big teeth. Allison draws her puppy with white colored pencil. She looks over at my paper.

"Fill up your paper," she says. "That's what the teacher said."

I never heard Ms. Simmons say that. On top of the picture I write, I am thankful for the mini cereal boxes.

Ms. Simmons is walking around our classroom. She looks at my picture and smiles. "It's nice and spacious, not too cluttered," she says. Then she whispers, "I like mini cereal boxes, too. You can use the box for a bowl if you want."

"You can?"

She nods. "It comes in handy when you're camping." When we're done, Ms. Simmons collects our papers. She says that she hopes we all have a nice Thanksgiving, and that she'll see us after the holiday break.

There is lots of traffic. People are picking up their kids to go visit grandparents. My grandparents are far away in China and in San Francisco, so we can't go there for just a short visit.

Ray holds out his sign and the

cars stop. "Don't eat too much pumpkin pie," he says, "or you'll come back looking roly-poly like me."

"You aren't roly-poly," I say.

He pats his stomach. "The missus says I'm starting my diet. After Thanksgiving, that is."

"The missus" sounds so funny.

Laura catches up to me. She is kicking a sweet gum ball. "Hey," she says. "What are you doing for Thanksgiving?"

I have to think fast. We aren't having turkey because we like duck with honey and soy sauce better. I'm probably going to read at least one new library book every day. "I don't know yet. I think my mom's going to take her driver's test."

"What?"

"She's trying to get her driver's license."

"My mom's had hers forever," Laura says. She takes a deep breath. "We're going to Michigan," she says. "And we're taking Allison with us." She looks at me sideways. "Sorry. My mom said I could only take one friend." She takes a deep breath. "And you know how

Allison is. If I didn't invite her, I bet she'd never talk to me again."

I don't really care how Allison is. I could tell that to Laura but she won't stop talking. "We have these to-boggans," she says. "You know, the old-fashioned kind of sleds that go really fast."

I don't care about sleds and toboggans. I want to go home and read my new library book that has a picture of a small girl with a big sky on the front. I have it in my book bag and I could take it out and read-walk right now.

"Have you ever been to Michigan?" Laura asks.

I've never been to Michigan and I never want to go. I shake my head.

"Maybe next year I can invite you." She kicks the sweet gum ball into the street.

If she wanted to, Laura could have told her mother that she wanted to invite me, not Allison. But she didn't. It doesn't matter because I would not want to sleep in somebody else's bed for three nights without Mom and Dad and Ken. And Laura and her brothers fight all the time. Anyway who knows about next year?

I don't say anything. I'm trying to walk faster than Laura but she's trying hard to keep up. Then she says, "Or maybe next year I can stay with you over Thanksgiving."

"We don't go anywhere."

"That's okay. Andrew and David are mean and they won't ever let me have a ride on the toboggan. And my mom and dad are always fighting. So if I want to stay at your house next year, can I?"

I don't know what to say. I'm not much for sleepovers, and neither is Mom. She says in China, she never heard of children sleeping at friends' houses.

"We don't have turkey," I say finally.

"What do you have?"

"Duck."

"Do you eat with chopsticks at your house?"

"Sometimes."

"On Thanksgiving?"

"Maybe."

"I know how to eat with chopsticks and I like duck

better than turkey anyway. What do you have for breakfast?"

"Cereal."

"Don't you have something Chinese?"

"Just cereal," I say again.

"I like cereal," she says. "Can I come?"

Laura's eyes are begging. We are almost at the corner where she turns one way, and I turn the other. "Next year isn't for a long time," I say.

Seven

Get Well Soon

After Thanksgiving break, Allison brings pictures to school that she has put into a small album. At sharing time, she shows them to the class. *Laura and Allison on the toboggan,* it says under the first picture. They are both wearing red snowsuits and smiling at the camera. *Ice fishing,* says another. They are standing in the middle of a lake with fishing poles.

"I'd be scared to stand on that ice," Devon says.

"Me too," says Lucy.

"Not me," says Laura. "We went fishing almost every day." She looks at Allison.

"I caught a big bass," Allison says.

Allison passes the album around so we can see it better. I look closely at each of the pictures. Laura and Allison and the boys are building an igloo. It would be fun to build an igloo out of ice bricks. Laura's brothers are laughing. The last picture shows Laura and Allison asleep in the car on the way home.

Even if Laura had invited me, I probably wouldn't have gone. I didn't even really want to go trick-or-treating with her. Maybe that's why she picked Allison instead of me to go to Michigan. *You know how Allison is,* she said. Allison is a skinny girl with brown hair and sweater sets. Now she's whispering something to Lucy and looking sideways at Laura. She's a whispering kind of girl.

I feel like crying but I don't even know why because who cares about Michigan and toboggans? I want to take *Hush* out of my book bag and read but we're supposed to write about what we did over Thanksgiving. I don't know what to write. I played concentration with Ken and Dad. I read *My Louisiana Sky* twice because it was really good. I read *Charlotte's Web* out loud to Ken. On Thanksgiving, we had dinner at Auntie Linda's house with fish and duck and eel. Camille and I had fun playing with tangrams. First you cut a square into seven shapes. Then you use

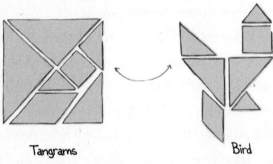

Tangrams   Bird

those shapes to make new pictures. After that, Camille's mom taught us how to knit. On Saturday, I went with Mom to Mr. Shepherd's and helped him reorganize his bookshelf. What is there to write?

Ms. Simmons is sitting at her desk, rubbing her face with her hands. Then I see that she has dark circles under her eyes. I go up to her desk. "I don't know what to write," I say.

"Whatever you want, Anna."

"What about your Thanksgiving?" I ask.

"My mother's been sick," she says.

I go back to my seat and think I'll make a card for Ms. Simmons's mother, but I don't know her name, so I have to ask.

"Olga," says Ms. Simmons. She seems impatient, but I can't make a card without knowing her name. "Olga Simmons."

Olga. What a funny name for Ms. Simmons's mother. To Mrs. Simmons, I write on the front. Get Well Soon.

"Is Ms. Simmons sick?" Laura whispers.

"It's not for her."

Laura looks confused.

"It's for Ms. Simmons's mother," I say.

"I thought we were supposed to write about our Thanksgiving."

"I'm making a card for Ms. Simmons's mother first."

Laura makes a much nicer card than mine. She draws a bright red house with a tree in front. She decorates the tree with candles. "That's what they did for Christmas trees in the olden days," she whispers. Then she writes:

Dear Ms. Simmons,

I'm sorry to hear that you were sick.
I hope you feel better soon.

Sincerely yours,
Laura A. Morgan

P.S. Merry Christmas.

Her cursive writing is perfect. My letters are slanting uphill. I can start over but there isn't enough time because I still have to write about my Thanksgiving before the bell rings for gym.

The gym teacher is absent and the substitute says we can have a free period. The kids are cheering and clapping. Some of them are shooting baskets and some are kicking the soccer ball. Tai keeps running up and tagging me. "Can't catch me," he says. But I don't feel like trying to catch him. Allison and Lucy are jumping rope. When the substitute isn't looking, I head to the locker room to get my book.

There on the bench is Laura, and she's been crying.
"What are you doing down here?" I ask.

She doesn't answer.

I sit down on the bench. "What's wrong?"

Laura's blond hair falls forward. "She hates me,"
Laura whispers.

"Who?"

"Allison." She swallows. "And everybody."

"I don't hate you," I say.

Laura takes a deep breath and looks up. "Allison said she and Lucy don't like me anymore."

I know I should say that's not true, but how do I know? Allison and Lucy were whispering today and looking over at Laura.

"I'm not like you are," she whispers. "You're so . . . I don't know." She smoothes back her hair. "You're tough."

"Not really."

"You seem like you are."

I look at the floor. "I just like to read."

We hear other kids coming. "Thanks," Laura says.

"For what?" I ask.

Laura grabs my hand. "For being my friend."

I squeeze her fingers. The locker room door opens. Laura goes over to the sink to wash her face and get a drink. By the time all the girls are there, you can hardly tell she was upset.

I stay after school to finish my card. The writing is crooked and the paper is dirty from erasing. I take out a new clean piece of paper.

Ms. Simmons is on the phone. She says, "No, Mother doesn't like coffee. Yes, she prefers tea. Yes, tea with lemon. I'll be over soon." She hangs up and rubs her eyes.

I draw a teacup with steam coming out. Next to it I draw a bright yellow lemon. On the cup I write *Get Well Soon,* and I sign my name in cursive.

Then I work on my Thanksgiving paragraph.

Over Thanksgiving, I read My Louisiana Sky. I think it is one of the best books I have ever read. I never thought of what it would be like if your mother was mentally retarded. At first the girl wished she had a normal mother, but then she realized that she loved her mother the way she was.

Writing that makes me think about Mom. I always wished I had a mom who spoke perfect English and who got her driver's license when she turned sixteen. But if Mom wasn't the way she is, she wouldn't be my mom and I wouldn't be me. Suddenly I just want to go home, but I have to finish my work first.

The other thing that happened was that my mom just passed her driver's test. She failed the first time but she passed the second. We celebrated on Thanksgiving.

Ms. Simmons is grading our spelling tests. I stand by her desk. "For your mother," I say, handing her the card.

"Thank you, Anna," she says. "Lemon tea, her favorite. How did you know?"

"I heard you on the telephone."

"You have good ears," she says.

I give Ms. Simmons my Thanksgiving paragraph and she reads it quickly. "I don't know that book, Anna, but I'll take it out of the library." Then she says, "Please congratulate your mom for passing the driver's test. You know, I failed that test three times."

"You did?"

She nods. "I finally passed on my fourth try."

As soon as I am outside, I take *Hush* out of my backpack. Toswiah has to change her name because of the witness protection program. I would hate to change my first name, but I wouldn't mind changing my last. Instead of Anna Wang, I could be Anna Brown or Anna Smith. I see my reflection in the glass pane in the door. But then my name wouldn't match my face. There is a girl in the Chinese class named April Sawalasky. She was adopted from China, so she has a Chinese face without a Chinese name. I wonder if she even thinks about that.

I close my book at the intersection. Ray has already gone home. I stand waiting for the cars to pass. The wind is blowing the leaves around. Finally there is a break in the traffic. I cross the street as fast as I can without running.

When I get to the corner, I see a blond girl up ahead with two taller boys. When I get closer, I see that it's Laura and her brothers. For a second I think maybe I should run to see how she is doing. She could come over and we could make lemonade. But she's with her brothers and the three of them seem just fine. I turn the other way and read-walk all the way home.

Eight

Winter Break

$\mathcal{I}$ get a book out of the library that has patterns and directions for paper airplanes. Dad brings home some thin cardboard from the store that's just perfect. I draw the pattern pieces onto the cardboard and cut them out carefully with small scissors. Then I fold the small tabs and glue the pieces together. It takes a long time, but I like seeing how the plane takes shape.

"Cool," Ken says. "I like that one." He points to the jet on the cover.

"That's the one I'm making," I say.

I finish it after lunch. Then I stand on the sofa and throw it across the living room. It takes a quick nose dive into the floor.

"According to the directions, it's supposed to make a loop," I say.

Ken picks it up and straightens out the nose. Dad thinks maybe we should bend the tail up more. I throw the airplane again. It takes a small dip and lands underneath our Christmas tree.

"Better," Ken says.

By the end of the day, we have three airplanes and all of them make a loop before landing. I finally realized that you have to make the tail fins a little wider. I think this is going to be the best winter break ever.

Then the phone rings. "It's Laura," Mom says.

I take the receiver. "Want to come over?" she asks.

"When?"

"Right now."

I don't want to go, but I can't just say that I'm busy making paper airplanes with my brother and my dad. I have to think of something fast. "I can't," I say. "I have to study Chinese characters for Chinese school tomorrow."

Laura doesn't say anything at first. "How about tomorrow? Can you come after Chinese school?"

I don't know what to say. Laura is waiting. "Okay. I'll come."

Mom wants to drive us to Chinese school by herself.

"Are you sure you don't want me to go along?" Dad asks.

Mom nods. "I can do it," she says, picking up the keys.

Mom drives a little slower than the other cars, but she stays in the middle of the road pretty well.

When we get to Chinese school, Camille and Auntie

Linda are standing by the curb. "Congratulations!" Auntie Linda shouts to Mom. "You are driving by yourself." Then they start talking a mile a minute in Chinese.

Camille looks at me. I notice that she has on a sweater that looks handmade. "I like your sweater," I say.

"My mom knitted it," she says. "It's freezing out here. You want to go in?"

Camille sits next to me on the floor of the basement room. "Are you in fourth grade?" I ask.

"Yup."

"What school do you go to?"

"Pleasant Hill. But we're moving at the end of the school year."

"Where to?"

"North Fairmount."

"Hey, that's where I go." Without even thinking, I grab her arm. "Maybe we'll be in the same class."

"But I think I might have to . . . I mean, I might be repeating." Her eyes meet mine. "My mom says you're really smart."

I think of how nice it will be to have Camille on the playground before school even if she's not in my class.

"I can introduce you to Ray."

"Who's he?"

"The crossing guard."

Teacher Zhen comes in. "Good morning, students," she says in Chinese. Then she says that we're going to learn words about winter like snow and ice and cold. I realize that I'm starting to understand what she says.

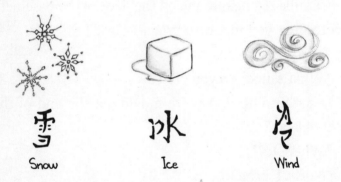

Snow   Ice   Wind

On the way home, Mom says that Auntie Linda told her that Camille is having trouble in school, mostly with reading. The teacher said she might have a learning disability.

"Camille said she's going to North Fairmount next year," I say.

Mom nods. "They think it will be a better school for her. She can have more help at North Fairmount than at Pleasant Hill."

"She's repeating fourth grade," I say.

"Maybe," Mom says. "They're not sure yet. Now she has a tutor."

As soon as we pull up in front of the house, I remember that I told Laura I was coming over after Chinese class. I wish I was going to Camille's house instead.

Maybe I'm getting a virus, some kind of flu. I can't go to Laura's house if I'm sick. I wouldn't want to infect the whole family with a bug. But I think of Laura's crying face in the locker room, and I know she is waiting.

I put the airplane book and a bunch of paper and scissors in a bag to take to Laura's. "I'm sure they have things to do there," Mom says, but I want to take my supplies. Mom walks down the hill with me.

We are almost at Laura's house. "I might not stay long," I tell Mom.

"Okay."

"I might just stay for half an hour."

Mom sighs. "Give Laura a chance."

I want to say I've given her and Allison and Lucy lots of chances. I want to say that Laura only wants to be my friend when Allison is mean to her. But Laura's mom is opening the door.

"Come in," she says to Mom. She has blue begging eyes just like Laura, and light brown hair that's flying around her face.

"Thank you," Mom says. "I have a test tomorrow. So I cannot stay."

Laura's mom nods. "Laura told me you are studying to be a nurse. How wonderful."

Laura motions to me from behind the stairs. "Let's spy," she whispers.

We go into the closet and look through a crack in the floor, but all I can see is light. There are winter coats and dresses hanging all around and the closet is hot and stuffy. Laura has a notebook to write down anything that we see. "Hey," she whispers, putting her eye to the crack. "Look."

I look but there is nothing to see.

In the notebook she writes, *David's arm*.

I didn't see any arm. I look again and this time I smell something funny. I inhale deeply. "What's that?" I whisper.

Laura sniffs. "I don't smell anything."

I sniff again. "It smells sweet."

"My mom's detergent, I bet," she whispers. But the smell isn't like that. It's getting stronger. Laura puts her eye to the crack again. She opens her mouth and covers it with her hand. Then she bursts out of the closet yelling, "Mom, they're starting a fire."

Her mother comes running from the kitchen. I follow Laura to the top of the stairs. Her mother goes quickly down to the basement. We stand crouched on the landing.

"Haven't you ever smelled incense before?" Andrew shouts.

Laura's mom is throwing the incense into the sink. The boys are saying all kinds of bad words to their mother. They say they know why their father doesn't want to live here anymore. Laura is writing furiously in the notebook.

I want to run home and make airplanes with Ken. I tell Laura we should go outside but she insists on writing everything down.

"What for?" I ask.

"Documentation," she says.

"What's that?"

"Evidence."

"What for?"

"In case we have to go to court again," she whispers.

"For burning incense?"

"Shhh," Laura says, turning the page.

Finally the boys are sent to their rooms for the rest of the day. Laura's mom fixes lunch and acts like nothing happened. After lunch, we go up to Laura's room and make a maze out of building blocks. She wants to put her gerbils in to see if they can find their way out.

"That's mean," I say.

"They like it," she says, picking one of them up by its tail because that's how you're supposed to pick up gerbils.

"Pick up the other one," she says. "We can race them."

I shake my head.

"They won't hurt you," she says.

Suddenly the gerbil bites her thumb. She drops it on the floor and it runs behind the bookcase.

"It doesn't really hurt," she says, putting her finger in her mouth.

We go into the bathroom and get a Band-Aid. "We better put some Bactine on," I say, "in case the gerbils have rabies."

"They don't," Laura says, putting the Band-Aid around her thumb.

"How are we going to catch the gerbil now?" I ask, hearing scratching noise coming from behind the bookcase.

"Let's just leave it," she says.

We go outside and climb in the mulberry tree. Laura

says that when Allison came over, she didn't want to climb the tree because it would get her white pants dirty. "Then she said she was bored at my house and she wanted me to ask my mom if we could use her makeup." Laura's eyes are getting watery. "She said if I didn't ask, she would go home."

"Did you ask?"

Laura shakes her head. "My mom doesn't even have makeup."

"Neither does my mom." Suddenly there's something I have to know. "Why do you invite Allison over to your house?"

"Each time she comes, I hope she'll be nice." Laura wipes her face with her sleeve. "I know you don't like her, but sometimes she's nice."

"Not most of the time."

"Nobody's nice all the time," Laura says.

I reach for the next branch and pull myself around. From there, I can see the whole neighborhood all the way to our school. I know what Laura means. Even Ms. Simmons gets irritated sometimes.

David and Andrew come out even though they're supposed to still be in their rooms. They are making some kind of tennis ball shooter with two big springs on the sides that's pretty neat. I think maybe I can launch one of my airplanes from it when it's done.

Laura is telling me that her mom is looking for another job because she lost the first one.

"You mean the typing one?" I ask.

Laura nods. "She had this terrible boss."

Then David says, "Do you guys want to help?" He lets us hammer in some of the nails for the crossbow.

When Mom comes to get me, Laura's mother says she thinks we had a nice time.

"Can you come back tomorrow?" Laura asks.

"I don't think so," I say quickly.

She looks sad. Then her face lights up. "If David and Andrew finish the tennis ball thing, I'll call you."

Nine

Spending the Night

$\mathcal{I}$t's after ten o'clock and I'm in bed reading *A Wrinkle in Time*. The librarian at school gave it to me. I don't usually like science fiction books but this one is different. Meg reminds me of me and Charles Wallace is a lot like Ken. The phone rings, and I hear Mom say, "Okay, yes, I understand. Yes, of course, no problem." When she hangs up, she says, "Laura is coming over."

But it's late and I have my pajamas on. "Right now?"

"Their family is having problems," Mom says.

"What problems?"

"I don't know the details, but Laura will stay with us for a few days."

"What about her brothers?"

"They're going to one of David's friends, but Laura doesn't want to go there."

My stomach drops. Even a few hours seems like a long time when someone comes to our house. What will I do with Laura for a few days? This is winter break. I want to make the airplanes in the book with Ken and read all the novels I took out of the library. On Christmas day, we'll open our presents in the morning, and then we'll have dinner with Auntie Linda and some of the other families from Chinese school.

"How many days is Laura staying?" I ask.

"As long as they need us," Mom says.

"What if she's still here on Christmas?"

"I don't think she'll be here so long. But if she is, she'll come with us to Auntie Linda's."

I sit up in bed and my book falls to the floor. "I don't see why she doesn't call Allison," I say. "She invited Allison to go to Michigan with them over Thanksgiving."

"Anna, that is not our business," Mom says. "Her mother asked us a favor. We will try to help."

Laura is carrying a small black bag and her eyes are all red. She stands in the doorway of my room.

"We have two fold-up mattresses," I say. "Do you want the red one or the blue one?"

"Blue," Laura says, looking at the sleeve of her blue striped pajamas.

I go into Ken's room, get the mattress out from underneath his bed, drag it into my room, and open it up on the floor.

"Where's your brother?" Laura asks.

"Spending the night at his friend's house. As usual."

Laura pushes the mattress over closer to my bed. I open the linen closet and take out a sheet, purple with blue dots. "That's pretty," she says, helping me spread it on top of the mattress. I find a pillow and a pillow-case and a blanket. When the bed is ready, Laura lies down and pulls the covers up to her chin.

I go back to bed and open *A Wrinkle in Time* but my eyes keep moving over the same words without knowing what they are saying. I hear the front door close so I know Laura's mother has left. Then Mom and Dad are in the kitchen, putting the dishes away. I could ask Laura about her parents, but maybe she doesn't want to talk about it. Her eyes are closed but I don't think she is asleep.

Tomorrow is Saturday. There is no Chinese school because of winter break. My stomach drops. Saturday is Mom's cleaning day. Ken will still be at Michael's. Laura and I can stay home by ourselves. But what will we do all day long?

Laura is lying perfectly still. Then I see that the pillowcase has darker spots where her tears have landed.

"What's wrong?" I whisper.

"My dad's not supposed to come over to our house anymore." She swallows. "But he comes anyway."

"And then what?"

"My mom won't let him in." She is crying and talking at the same time. "So he just waits there."

"For how long?"

"I don't know. A long time."

A car goes down the street and the headlights shine

on the wall. Laura sits up. "Do your mom and dad fight?" she asks.

"They argued a lot when my mom was learning how to drive."

"I hope my dad didn't see me come over here," Laura says. She looks around. "You have a ton of books."

"They're mostly Christmas presents," I say. "Do you want to read?"

She shakes her head.

"Do you want me to read you *A Wrinkle in Time*?"

She lies back down. "Sure."

I start at the beginning or else Laura won't understand what's going on. She's really quiet while I read. Later Mom comes up, and then Dad. They don't tell me to turn off my light like they usually do. I read through chapter six. Finally when I think Laura is asleep, I look over at the mattress. With her eyes closed, her face looks soft.

I hear the doorbell ring. Who would be coming to our house this late? Laura must be a deep sleeper because she doesn't move. I hear Dad go to the front

door and turn on the porch light. I tiptoe to the top of the stairs just as Dad opens the door.

"I am Mr. Morgan," a man's voice says.

I hold my breath. Dad does not invite him in. "Can I help you?" he asks.

"I've come to get my daughter," he says.

"I'm sorry. You must have come to the wrong house," Dad says.

The man stands there for a minute. "I'm sorry," he says.

Dad closes the door. I hear the man's footsteps on our front steps, and when I look out the window, he is getting into his car.

My heart is beating so hard I can feel it in my throat. Then I run down the stairs into the living room. Mom and Dad are sitting next to each other on the sofa and I climb onto Mom's lap like a baby. Dad rubs my back with his warm hands.

"The family is having trouble," Mom says.

"Maybe he just missed his daughter," Dad says.

"Then why did you tell him he had the wrong house?"

Dad is quiet for a minute. "I wasn't really sure what to do. Mom told me that Laura's mother asked us to take care of her, so that is what we should do."

"Poor Laura," Mom says. "Family trouble is not easy." Mom puts my hair behind my ears like she used to when I was little. "You're tired, Anna," she says. "Time to sleep."

❊ ❊ ❊

Laura's blond hair is spread all over the pillow. When I tiptoe past her mattress, she moves, but she doesn't wake up.

I turn onto my side and stare at the cracks in the

paint on the wall. In Chinese class, the cracks are big like rivers, but here they are thin like a spider web or a wrinkle in time. One crack goes into the next into the next until they fade into the wall. Maybe tomorrow Laura and I can play that tangrams shapes game. We can cut the shapes out of cardboard and try to make pictures out of them like I did with Camille. That would be something Laura would like to do.

Chapter Ten

Saturday

We have Corn Pops for breakfast.

"I thought you guys had those small cereal boxes," Laura says.

"Only once in a while."

"Do you eat with chopsticks?"

"You can't eat cereal with chopsticks," I say.

Laura pours herself a big bowl and covers it with milk. Mom always tells us not to take more than we can eat, but when Laura leaves half of the cereal and milk in her bowl, Mom doesn't say anything.

After breakfast, Mom says, "You two can stay home while I go clean the apartments." I wish she wouldn't have said that about cleaning, but it's too late now. She goes down to the basement to get her cleaning supplies.

"I like to clean," Laura says. "Can we go?"

"My mom does the cleaning."

"You said she cleans in one of those high-rises, right?"

I nod.

"I've never been up there." Laura looks down. "Where's your dad?"

"At work."

"I don't want to stay here alone," she says quickly.

"I thought you and Allison stay alone all the time."

Laura's eyes get watery. "Not anymore."

Mom comes up with her bucket full of supplies. "We want to go with you," I say.

She looks surprised. "Mr. Shepherd will be happy. Now hurry so we don't miss the bus."

The wind is strong and snow flurries are blowing around. We zip our jackets all the way up. Laura's has a hood but it won't stay on so Mom ties her scarf around Laura's head. I pull my hat down almost to my eyes. The bus comes as soon as we get to the stop.

"I've only ridden the bus once before," Laura says.

"In your whole life?"

"Yup. My mom drives us everywhere."

We introduce Laura to Mrs. Lukens. She gives us each two thin mints.

Laura smiles as the elevator goes up. "I love that feeling in my stomach," she says. "Just like a roller coaster."

When the door opens, Mr. Shepherd is waiting for us. "Now, who's this?" he asks when he sees Laura.

"Laura Morgan," I say.

He holds out his hand. Laura looks like she's afraid to shake hands with a man in a wheelchair, but finally she does.

"I've set some things aside for you," he says, wheeling himself ahead of us into the apartment. In the middle of the living room is a big cardboard box. "Take a look."

The box is full of scraps of fabric. "Wow," Laura says, picking up a piece of blue silk and waving it around. "I bet my mom would really like this."

"It's yours for the taking," Mr. Shepherd says.

"Where did you get all this material?" I ask.

"Mrs. Shepherd used to sew up a storm," he says.

He watches us rummage through the box. Then he wheels himself over to the window and reads the newspaper in the sunshine.

Laura and I sort the fabrics into the ones we like a lot, the ones we sort of like, and the ones we don't like at all.

Mr. Shepherd moves himself into the bedroom.

"Where's he going?" Laura whispers.

"He usually takes a nap about now."

We keep on sorting and talking. "I wish I could sew," Laura says.

"It's not that hard."

"Can you teach me sometime?"

"Yup," I say, picking up a piece of black velvet.

"I'm going to ask my mom if we can get a sewing machine for Christmas," she says. "But I bet she'll say no." Laura puts a piece of orange fabric around her head like a headband. "Now that they're splitting up, there's not that much money." She sees Mom scrubbing the kitchen floor. "Do you think your mom gets paid a lot?"

"I don't know."

The afternoon goes by so fast, we can hardly believe it when Mom says she'll run down and help Mrs. Watson for a few minutes, and then it will be time to go home.

"This is fun," Laura says. "Can I come with you next Saturday?"

"If you want to," I say.

"It's peaceful with your family," she says.

"I fight with Ken sometimes," I say.

Suddenly we hear a loud bang like something is falling. Laura looks at me. "What was that?"

"Mr. Shepherd?" I call.

"No problem," he says. "I'm just a little clumsy."

I open the bedroom door, and Mr. Shepherd is sitting on the edge of the bed. "I lost my balance there for a minute," he says, wiping his forehead with a handkerchief. He has a small cut above his eye where he fell against the headboard.

Laura puts her hand to her mouth. "Are you okay?"

"A little cut never did much harm."

"We better go get your mom," Laura says.

Mr. Shepherd waves his hand. "No need to bother Mary. She tells me to stay put, but do I listen?" He shakes his head. "Anna, wet this handkerchief for me, will you, please?"

I run it under cold water, wring it out, and give it back to Mr. Shepherd.

"A little coldness can go a long way," he says. "Now, let me tell you what I was after. You see that basket there on the floor?" He looks at Laura. "Get that for me, will you, please, and set it up here on the bed."

Laura gets the basket and Mr. Shepherd opens the top. "Needles, pins, thread, scissors. You girls take whatever it is you need. Take the whole basket. It's not doing much good here gathering dust."

While Mr. Shepherd takes a nap, Laura and I sit on the living room floor with the basket between us. There are lots of spools of thread of all different colors, a pin cushion full of needles, a box of snaps, a roll of Velcro, several zippers.

"He bumped his head getting this sewing basket for us," Laura says.

I nod. "Mr. Shepherd hates to ask for help."

"I'm like that, too," Laura says. She picks up the blue fabric. "I think my mom will really like a scarf out of this." She winds it around her wrist. "It's so soft and silky."

Mom comes back in. "Time to go home now," she says, gathering her cleaning supplies.

Laura is looking out the big window at the river.

"Mr. Shepherd is really nice," she says.

Mom tiptoes over to the bedroom and opens the door. "Looks like he cut himself."

"He knocked it on the headboard," I say.

Mom shakes her head. "I told him to ask when he needs something."

"He was getting the sewing basket," I say. "For us."

It's already dark as we walk to the bus stop. Laura takes a deep breath. "Smells like snow," she says.

I sniff. The air is damp.

"You want to go sledding tomorrow?" Laura asks.

I want to make more airplanes with Ken and I want to read my new book. Anyway, it might not snow. But it has been fun having Laura around.

"Do you?" she asks again.

"If it snows," I say, stepping onto the bus.

"It will," Laura says. "I can tell." She scoots in next to me on the seat. "I can't wait to give my mom the silk fabric."

Eleven

Christmas

$\mathcal{L}$aura's mom comes early on Sunday. "Thank you very much," she says to Mom. "I can't tell you how much we appreciate your help."

"Laura can come anytime," Mom says.

Laura holds on to her mother's arm. "Can we get a sewing machine?"

"We'll see," her mother tells her.

"Anna's going to teach me how to sew," Laura says. Then she feels around in her pocket. "I lost it," she says to me.

"What?"

"The silk," she whispers into my ear. "Remember?"

We run upstairs, but it's not there. Laura looks really upset. "If I find it, I'll call you," I say.

I search the house, but the blue silk isn't anywhere. Maybe it fell out of Laura's pocket when we got off the bus.

I finish *A Wrinkle in Time* and start *The Prince and the Pauper* about two boys who switch places. I wonder what it would be like to switch places with Laura. What would it be like to have your parents split up? And what would Laura do if she were me? I don't think she'd like Chinese school. She wouldn't understand a thing. And it would be strange for her to be with all Chinese kids. But then, she always seems so interested in Chinese stuff.

When Ken gets home, we make three more airplanes, so that brings our fleet to nine. If we throw them gently with the nose tipped down a little, they loop. When Dad comes, we have a contest to see whose can loop the best. We're so busy with our airplanes that we almost forget tomorrow is Christmas.

"Can I spend the night in your room?" Ken asks.

"What for?"

"So you won't wake up before me and open your presents."

"You know we have to wait for Mom and Dad anyway," I say.

"The blue mattress is already in your room," he says, running to get his pillow.

I can't believe I got the whole set: *A Wrinkle in Time, A Wind in the Door, A Swiftly Tilting Planet,* and *Still Waters.* Mom and Dad always know exactly which books are my favorites. I want to start reading the second one right away, but Ken is hopping around like a jumping bean. "Don't read now, Anna. Please." He is grabbing my arm. "First let's go downstairs."

Mom and Dad lead us to the basement, where there are two brand-new silver scooters with bows on the handlebars. We race around the furnace until we're totally dizzy. Ken tries all kinds of fancy tricks like riding on one wheel. Then he wants to ride outside but it's too cold.

Dad and I start folding wontons to take to Auntie Linda's when the phone rings. I think it's going to

How to Fold a Won Ton

1. Fill   2. Fold   3. Pinch   4. Done!

be Laura because it finally snowed and I know she wanted to go sledding, but it's Camille. She says her mom told her I was good at writing, and she wonders if I can help her with a biography report that she has to turn in after break.

"About who?" I ask.

"George Washington Carver," she answers.

"Sure. Come on over."

Camille has perfect handwriting, but her report is too short and she has lots of words spelled wrong, like she wrote *wood* instead of *would* and *are* instead of *our*.

We look through the biography she brought, and it talks about all the different things you can make out of peanuts. "You could write about how to make oil and soap," I say.

It takes Camille a long time to write one more paragraph and she doesn't know how to spell lots of words. When she's finally done, she asks me if I like North Fairmount Elementary.

"It's okay," I say. "I really like my teacher, Ms. Simmons, and the other teacher, Mr. Schmitz, is pretty nice too. And then there's the crossing guard, Ray."

"What about the kids?"

I shrug. "They're okay. But they're not really my friends. I mean . . . they go back and forth."

Camille nods. "I know what you mean. I have a friend Beth at my school. But sometimes she thinks what I say is stupid." Camille looks down at her paper. "I hope I'll do better at your school than at mine. My mom says they have lots of services, like a reading van and everything." Her face is wide and open, as if she doesn't mind telling the whole world what she's bad at.

"My handwriting isn't half as good as yours."

Camille smiles. "We'd make a good team. You read and I write."

❋ ❋ ❋

When we eat dinner at Auntie Linda's, Camille wants to sit next to me. After dinner, all of us kids play tangrams and charades and Twister. I can hardly believe it when Mom says it's time to go home.

Twelve

Icicles

Sunday night the wind picks up. In the morning, it's twelve degrees and there's a layer of ice on everything. We turn on the radio. School is on plan B, which means we start an hour later than usual. I hope Ray listens to the radio.

Ken grabs his jacket and hurries outside to meet Michael. They are slipping and sliding in the driveway. I read *A Wind in the Door* for half an hour before heading to school.

I take two icicles carefully off the stone wall where the poison ivy was.

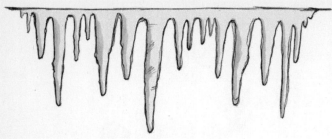

"Can you get poison ivy even in winter?" I ask Ray when I get to school.

He thinks so.

"From icicles?" I show him the two I found.

"Those won't hurt you. Now you better hurry. You only have about two minutes today."

I drop the icicles and cross the street.

Ms. Simmons asks us to write about what we did over winter break. Allison taps me on the shoulder. "We went skiing," she whispers. "What about you?"

"Nothing special," I say. I write about making paper airplanes. Ms. Simmons asks if anyone wants to read their paragraphs out loud. Laura raises her hand.

"I went with Anna to the apartment that her mom cleans," Laura reads. I can't believe Laura is telling that to the whole class! Allison is looking at me with a frown on her face. "This really nice man named Mr. Shepherd lives there. He has to use a wheelchair to move around but he does everything by himself. He gave us a bunch of fabric and a sewing basket when we left. Going to Mr. Shepherd's was the best part of my winter break."

I am counting the tiles on the floor. Brown, white, brown, white, then white, brown, white, brown. "Can I go with you guys next time?" Allison whispers.

I can't believe Allison wants to go to Mr. Shepherd's. I don't know what to say. Three kids might be too many for him and I don't really like Allison. But I know what it feels like to be the one not invited. "Maybe," I whisper.

When I get to the crosswalk, Ray has a huge icicle for me. "Wow, this is the biggest one I've ever seen," I say. "Thanks a lot."

Ray nods. "Can't say I've seen them get much bigger than that. I guess if we were to go to Alaska, we'd see some, but not around here."

I hold it carefully the whole way home so it won't

break. As soon as I get inside, I open the freezer. The icicle only fits in diagonally.

Mom looks up from her flashcards. "You still have the one from last year," she reminds me.

"I know. I'm saving it." I shut the freezer door.

We sit at the kitchen table and have my favorite bean paste, *bao zia,* for a snack. Then Ken goes back outside and Mom starts reading her biology book.

I go into my room. Mom's right, I do save everything. I still have the small acorns from Ray by my bed and the watercolors and the sewing basket from Mr. Shepherd, and a box of leftover yarn from Camille's mom. I find a blue knitted square. It would be perfect for a hat, I think, holding it around my head. I use a big needle to sew up the side. On top, I make a fluffy pom-pom.

In the morning, I run down the hill to show Ray my hat. But where is he? He's never been late.

Laura joins me at the curb. "Do you know where Ray is?" I ask.

She shakes her head.

Finally Miss Johnson, the playground monitor, comes out and helps us cross. I ask her if she knows anything about Ray but she hasn't heard. Ms. Simmons doesn't know either. All day I worry so much that I can hardly do my math problems. I take my library book out of my backpack, but my mind keeps thinking about Ray instead of the words on the page. Laura writes me a note with a sad face.

Maybe he's sick.

Mom says maybe Ray went to Florida for the rest of the winter, but I don't think so. He wouldn't miss schooldays for Florida. And he would have told us he was going.

I call the school to get his full name. Ray McAlister, the secretary says. I look in the telephone book. There is an R. McAlister at 3624 Whitaker Street. I put on my jacket, but I'm scared to go by myself. What if R. is not Ray?

Mom cannot come with me. She has to finish a lab report by tomorrow. Ken is outside with Michael. In my pocket is Laura's note with the sad face. All day she kept looking out the window just like me. I pick up the phone and call her.

"Want to go with me to Ray's house?" I ask her. "I think I found his address."

"Meet you at the corner," she says.

We walk the six blocks and ring the doorbell. A lady opens the door. "Excuse me. We're looking for Ray," I say, "the crossing guard."

There he is, all propped up on a hill of pillows. His leg is wound in a huge orange cast the color of his vest.

"Ray!" we shout, running right past Mrs. McAlister.

"How do you like the color?" Ray asks.

"It matches your vest," Laura says.

Ray tells us how he was getting another big icicle off the porch roof when he slipped and broke his leg. Mrs. McAlister shakes her head. "Raymond and his icicles." Laura looks at me and we giggle. We never knew he could be Raymond.

Ray notices my new hat. "Great thinking cap," he says. "Wish I had one myself."

"It might help," Mrs. McAlister says.

"How many minutes until you get the cast off?" I ask.

"A lot," Ray says.

Mrs. McAlister makes us hot apple cider. I tell Ray that Miss Johnson is not very good at helping us cross the street.

"She doesn't even know what time it is," Laura says.

"Now, that's a problem," Ray says. "Believe me, I'll be back to work in a couple of weeks."

"Raymond," Mrs. McAlister says in a warning voice. Ray looks at us and winks.

Thirteen

Sewing

The next time Laura comes over, all the snow has melted. We take out the sewing basket from Mr. Shepherd. Laura picks up a big piece of bright yellow fabric. "I bet Allison would like this," she says. "But she hardly talks to me anymore."

"Is she mad at you again?"

Laura shrugs. Then she picks up a piece of brown wool. "My dad has a suit like this." She looks up. "He has his own apartment now."

"Are your parents divorced?"

"Separated."

"Maybe they'll get back together."

Laura shakes her head. "All they do is fight." She holds up a big piece of orange fabric. "I wonder what Mrs. Shepherd was planning to make out of this?"

"Maybe a Halloween costume for one of their grandchildren," I say. Suddenly I have an idea. "Hey, we could make orange vests like Ray's to help kids cross the street."

"But we're not crossing guards," Laura says.

"I know, but we could help Miss Johnson."

First we measure ourselves and make patterns out of newspaper. Then we cut out the pieces and stitch them together at the shoulders. Finally we put them on and look into the mirror.

"Perfect," Laura says, dancing around the room.

"Is that an Irish dance?" I ask.

"Just a dance," she says, twirling me around.

In the morning, Laura and I get to the curb early. The sun is starting to rise behind the school building.

"Thank goodness I've got helpers today," Miss Johnson says.

Lucy and Allison are waiting to cross the street. "We have about six more minutes," I say, glancing at my watch.

Allison looks at our orange vests. "Are you two crossing guards?" she asks.

"Just substitutes," I say. "Until Ray gets back."

"Hey, Laura," Allison says. "Want to see my new belt?"

We both look at Allison, but you can't see her belt with her coat on.

"Come into the bathroom, and I'll show you," she says with her back to me. "It'll only take a second."

Miss Johnson stands in the street and we all cross.

"Are you coming?" Allison asks, looking only at Laura.

"Not now," Laura says.

"Now or never," Allison says. Then she grabs Lucy's hand and they hurry toward the building.

I look at Laura. Maybe I should tell her that she can go with them if she wants. I can help Miss Johnson until the bell rings, and after that I can read *A Wind in the Door*. But we sewed the orange vests together. We told Ray we would help Miss Johnson until he got back. And if Laura leaves, I will be alone.

Laura is looking at her watch. "We have five more minutes," she says.

On Friday after school, Laura and I stop by Ray's. He has gotten pretty good at getting around in the wheelchair, and he has a cast he can walk on, too. "Only problem is my toes get cold," he says.

"How many more minutes until you can cross us again?" I ask.

Ray looks at the clock. "I'd say about nine hundred."

Quickly I divide by sixty. "That's only fifteen hours from now."

"That's tomorrow morning!" Laura says.

"You got it," says Ray.

"I think you might be pushing it, Raymond," Mrs. McAlister says.

At home I look through the yarn. There is another knitted square sort of like my hat, only smaller. I fold it in half and stitch up the side. There. That should work to cover Ray's toes. Mom helps me put a piece of elastic around the top to make sure it stays on. I put it into my book bag so I won't forget to take it to Ray tomorrow.

When I wake up, my room is strangely light.

"February snow," Mom says. "So heavy and wet."

I call Laura. "Want to visit Ray before school?" I ask her.

"Meet you at the corner!" she says.

I put on my boots.

"Isn't it too early to leave for school?" Mom asks.

"Laura and I have a stop to make on the way," I say.

Ray's kitchen light is on. I knock on the side door and he pulls the curtain back. When he sees us, he opens the door wide and hurries us in. "Hey, little ladies, so nice to see you before the sunrise."

I hold up the knitted sock. "Well if that isn't the perfect way to warm up my toes." Mrs. McAlister puts it over Ray's toes. "I'm warmer already," he says.

Ray's sock

Laura looks at the clock on the wall that's shaped like a house. "We better hurry," she says. "Only eleven more minutes."

Ray puts on his jacket. "Are you sure you're okay to go out in all this snow, Raymond?" Mrs. McAlister asks.

"Not to worry," he says. "I got my helpers today."

Ray leans on us and we step into the snow.

Fourteen

Absent

$\mathcal{L}$aura is not at school on Monday. Maybe she has a stomachache like she gets sometimes. She's not there on Tuesday, Wednesday, or Thursday either. I read *A Swiftly Tilting Planet* in two days. "Have you seen Laura?" Ms. Simmons asks me and Allison and Lucy.

None of us has.

"I wonder what happened to her," Allison says to me. "Her mom's weird, don't you think?"

I shrug. I don't really know Laura's mom. Mostly she just seems tired to me.

When I get home, Mom is making a noodle dish to

celebrate Chinese New Year. "Long noodles for a long life," she says.

"Laura has been absent all week," I say.

Mom dries her hands on a towel. "Let's walk to their house."

We ring the doorbell, but nobody answers and their car is gone.

"Do they have family here?" Mom asks.

"Her aunt. And she has more relatives in Michigan."

"Maybe they went there," Mom says.

I wonder what it would be like if they decided to stay in Michigan and I never saw Laura again. Thinking that makes my eyes water.

At home I look through the fabric scraps. There are some pieces that would be big enough for small drawstring bags like the one I made for my lunch bag. I cut out rectangles and lay them out in a row on the floor. I could match dark blue and light blue, but then it might look better with red. I wish Laura were here to help me decide. I don't really feel like sewing the bags without her.

Ken starts rearranging the fabric on the floor.

"Don't."

He tosses a handful of rectangles into the air. "They're just a bunch of rags."

"They are not," I say.

I look out the window. The sun is shining behind the branches of the mulberry tree outside my window. Soon the buds will get fat and the funny-shaped leaves will open. When the berries fall, Laura and I can collect them to make berry stew.

I take a piece of paper and on the top I write, Dear Laura, I hope you come home soon. From, Anna. Then I cut out tiny rectangles of fabric and glue them onto the bottom of the card. It's bright and cheerful, but it still needs something. I know. On the back I use my watercolors to write *peng you* in Chinese characters. Underneath I write the meaning: friend.

朋友

Mom is at the dining room table, putting chocolate coins into special red envelopes that we get for Chinese New Year. "Can I have one of those envelopes?" I ask.

Mom hands me one with the Chinese character for happiness in gold on the front. I fold my card and stuff it into the envelope. Mom gives me a chocolate coin to go with it. Then I ride my scooter down to Laura's house and slip the red envelope underneath their door.

Fifteen

Staying Home

Saturday morning Mom gathers her cleaning supplies. "Are you coming with me today?" she asks.

I can't decide. Mr. Shepherd might be expecting me. But it's cold outside and I don't feel like getting dressed and it's not as fun there without Laura. Plus I have ten Chinese characters to learn for this afternoon. "I think I'll stay home," I tell Mom.

Mom is putting on her jacket. "Dad closed the store last night, so he's still asleep. When Ken wakes up, keep an eye on him until Dad wakes up."

I am just reaching for my book when the doorbell rings. I look out the window, and Laura is standing there without even a jacket on. I hurry to open the door.

"I thought you'd probably be cleaning with your mom," she says. "But I wanted to check just in case."

"I decided to stay home today." I grab her arms and practically pull her into the house. "It's freezing out there."

Laura is shivering so much that her teeth are chattering.

"Where's your jacket?" I ask.

"I left it at my cousin's house." Laura looks down. "My mom told me not to bother you so much. But I showed her the card you left for me and then she said I could come over. If you're not busy."

"I'm just reading."

I want to ask Laura why she wasn't at school all week, but her eyes are puffy and she's still shivering. We go into my room and cover ourselves with a blanket. Then I reach over to my bookshelf and take off some of my old picture books.

"Hey, I remember that book," she says, pointing to *George Shrinks*. "It used to scare me to death."

"Why?"

"I was afraid that maybe someday I'd shrink too," she says. "I still don't like it." She sets the book aside and picks up another one. "Hey, here's *Little Blue and Little Yellow.*"

We read it together.

"Remember how everyone thought we were a Visa card?" Laura asks.

"Except for Mr. Shepherd. Ken and I went over there with the costume, and he knew who we were."

"Why didn't you go with your mom today?" Laura asks.

"I have all these Chinese characters to learn. And I was too lazy to get dressed." I pause. "Plus it's not as fun at Mr. Shepherd's without you."

Laura smiles.

"Ms. Simmons was asking about you."

"We had to stay away for a few days."

I wait to see if Laura wants to tell me anything else.

"My mom was at her wits' end" is all she says.

"Are you hungry?" I ask.

"A little."

We go into the kitchen and have some cereal. After that I show Laura all the rectangles of fabric on the floor. She kneels next to me. "I like this dark purple with the light purple, don't you?"

I nod. "And this green with the black."

"Or maybe the yellow."

We mix and match the rectangles until they are just the way we want them. Then we take the thread out of the sewing basket and start sewing up the sides to make drawstring bags.

"This is hard," Laura says, looking at her uneven stitches. Her face looks like mine when I'm trying to write in cursive.

"It takes practice," I say.

We decide to make a production line. Laura cuts out more rectangles, I sew up the sides, she cuts the drawstrings, I make the casings. By the time Mom gets back, we have seven bags. Ray gets an orange one to match his vest. Mr. Shepherd's is blue and yellow like the book. Ms. Simmons gets a print with little bicycles all over it. Laura's mom gets bright blue to match her

Ray   Mr. Shepherd   My Mom

Ms. Simmons   Laura's Mom   Camille

eyes. My mom gets pink polka dots. I pick turquoise velvet for Camille. There is one bag left.

"For you," I say handing Laura the purple one.

"What about you?"

"I already have one, remember?"

Laura plays with the drawstring. "We drove to my aunt's in Michigan last week," she says. She looks out the window. "We figured my dad might follow us to your house, but he wouldn't follow us all the way to Michigan."

Mom says she has something for Laura in her pocket.

"What is it?" I ask.

Mom shows us the blue silk.

"Where was it?" Laura is smiling so wide.

"Mr. Shepherd found it at the bus stop."

"You mean he wheeled himself all the way there?" I ask.

Mom nods. "Once Mr. Shepherd has an idea, you can't change his mind."

Laura's mom calls and says it's time for her to come home. Outside it has started to rain, cold icy drops that hit the windowpanes.

"You can wear my jacket," I say.

"What if you want to go out?"

"I have another one."

"My aunt is going to mail mine back from Michigan," Laura says. She puts my jacket on and winds the blue silk scarf around her neck. "Now I feel like you," she says. "Hey, can you teach me the word for friend that you wrote on my card?"

"*Peng you*," I say.

"*Peng you*," she says, only instead of *pung yo*, it sounds like *penguin*. "Shee shee for being my penguin," she says.

I watch Laura through the window. From the back, you can't tell who it is. We're both small and skinny.

I wonder what it would be like if we really switched places like in *The Prince and the Pauper.*

I sit at my desk and copy the Chinese characters into the squares in the notebook. For some reason, learning to write in Chinese is easier than in English. It's more like drawing than writing to me. Teacher Zhen showed us how some characters actually come from pictures of real things. Like the one for cow really looks like a cow, if you look at it right. We're learning animals to go with the Chinese zodiac. Dog, cat, cow, horse, rooster, and rat. I copy them over and over again. This afternoon we'll learn six more animals, and then we're making Chinese zodiac calendars.

As soon as we get to Chinese class, Camille runs over to me with her arms in the air. "I got an A!" she says. "My first one ever."

"That's great," I say, looking at her report. "Are you still going to come to my school next year?"

Camille nods. "Fifth grade," she says, grinning.

The bell rings. Teacher Zhen is teaching us Chinese exercises. At first I feel kind of stupid touching my toes, but the exercises get more and more complicated. We mix up left and right and Camille bumps my head. We land in a heap on the floor laughing so hard, we can't stand up.

Sixteen

Persuasive Writing

The word of the week is *persuade,* and we're supposed to write persuasive paragraphs. "It's like *convince*," Ms. Simmons says. "What would you like to convince your parents of?"

Laura thinks for a minute. Then she writes the title in fancy script: *Bedtime*.

Allison shows us a little picture of her new puppy. "I'm trying to persuade my mom to let my puppy sleep in my bed, but she says dogs are dirty," she whispers.

"Girls, no talking," Ms. Simmons says.

I can't think of anything to write about. I already get to read until after ten o'clock and even later on weekends. I don't wish I had a puppy that slept in my bed. Ms. Simmons is walking around, looking at our work.

"Your paper is blank," she whispers.

"I can't think of anything."

"You will," Ms. Simmons says.

"Do we have to persuade our parents?" I ask.

"You can persuade anyone," she says.

I keep repeating that *persuasive* word and rolling it around in my mouth. I like the sound of it. *Persuade, persuasive, persuasively.* Finally I decide to write a letter to the principal of our school.

Dear Mrs. Robinson,

I know that sometimes teachers at our school loop so that they teach the same class for two years. Please let Ms. Simmons loop so that she will be our fifth grade teacher next year. There are many reasons. First, she already knows us. Second, she is a really, really good teacher. Third, she lets us read whatever books we want. Those are my reasons.

Sincerely yours,

Anna Wang

I fold the letter into a small square and write Mrs. Robinson on the outside. "Is it okay if I give my persuasive writing to Mrs. Robinson?" I ask. "Because it's about something very important."

"You've persuaded me," Ms. Simmons says.

At lunchtime, I deliver the note to Mrs. Robinson's mailbox.

In the afternoon, Ms. Simmons gives us each a long roll of paper to make timelines of our lives. We draw a line on the side of the roll with all the dates from the time we were born until now. For 1998 I write, I was born in Central Hospital on September 19, Year of the Dog.

Allison looks at my paper. "Year of the Dog?"

"In the Chinese zodiac," I say.

"Cool. That must be why I like dogs." She draws two puppies on her timeline and writes *Year of the Dog,* too. Most everyone in our class was born in 1998 so they all write *Year of the Dog* except for Richard and Lucy, who are Year of the Rooster.

I'm not sure what to write for the rest of the years. Not that much happened. For 2004 I draw a picture of a book because that's when I learned to read. For 2005, I draw Ray's crossing guard stop sign. For 2008, I write the word *China* in characters to show that I am learning Chinese.

中国

Then I draw a bunch of small book covers because this year I read a whole lot.

Laura brings her timeline over to show me. 2005,

the year I met Anna, it says with a smiley face. 2008, *my parents split up*. She draws a sad face.

Then I add something else to my timeline: a dot of blue and a dot of yellow with the touching part green. "To remember our Halloween costume," I say grabbing Laura's hand.

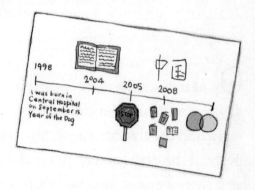

Seventeen

Spring Break

On March 22, we have a party to celebrate the first day of spring and the equinox, which means that the night and the day are equal. Ms. Simmons asks us to push all the desks and chairs to the back of the room, and then we play a game where you're supposed to get everyone to guess your word without saying it. My word is *sidewalk*. At first I try just walking around, but everyone just says walk, not sidewalk. Suddenly I have an idea. On the board, I write: *Where the ____ Ends*.

Laura waves her hand. "Sidewalk!" she says

We each get two points, and at the end, my team wins. Then we eat green Rice Krispies treats that Lucy's mom made, and chocolate eggs. Laura

and I give Ms. Simmons the drawstring bag and she loves it. "This will
be perfect for my lunch when I go on
bike rides," she says, hugging us both
at once.

Ms. Simmons gives each of us an
envelope. "Inside is your room assignment
for next year," Ms. Simmons says, "and your third-
quarter report cards. Please look it over at home with
your parents and bring it back after the break with a
signature."

I'm not worried about the report card because I
know I got all A's except for handwriting, but what
about my teacher for next year? The principal never
wrote me back. Maybe my letter didn't persuade her
of anything.

I really want to know who my teacher will be, so
I lift the flap and peek inside the envelope. *Sylvester,*
it says, whoever that is. Ms. Sylvester? Mr. Sylvester?
Could Sylvester be the first name? Maybe she's a young
new teacher with puffy hair. I might not like that
Ms. Sylvester at all. Maybe Mrs. Robinson never even

had time to read my letter, or maybe my ideas were not persuasive enough.

"We're not supposed to open the envelopes until we get home," Lucy says.

I look up. Laura is peeking at hers, too. "Who'd you get?" I whisper.

"Sylvester," she whispers. "Who's that?"

"Mine says Sylvester, too. I never heard of her," I say.

"Me either."

My stomach is starting to hurt, so I put my head down on my desk. Ms. Simmons slips me a note.

Dear Anna,

Thank you for the beautiful bag. Maybe Mr. Sylvester and I will use it to keep our special things. So far we have a seashell that we found in Florida and a fossil from a creek in Indiana. I hope you have a nice spring break.

Ms. Simmons

P.S. My mother thanks you for the card you
made her. She is feeling much better now.

There is that name Sylvester again. Ms. Simmons
looks at me and winks. "This summer I'm getting
married," she whispers.

"To Mr. Sylvester?" I can hardly believe it. "Who's
he?"

"Well, he's got his own ideas, Anna, like someone
else I know. And he loves to read. I think you two
would get along well."

"Does that mean you are looping?"

Ms. Simmons smiles. "You got it," she whispers.

Ray holds his arms out to stop the traffic like he does
every day. But instead of saying have a nice afternoon,
he says, "Have a nice spring break."

"We'll come visit you," I say, looking at Laura.

Ray smiles. "I sure hope so."

Ray limps as he walks to the curb. Then he reaches
into his pocket and takes out the orange drawstring bag.
"The misses uses it, too," he says. "We both thank you."

❊ ❊ ❊

Laura and I are kicking a sweet gum ball back and forth. When we get to the corner, she says, "David and Andrew finally finished the tennis ball launcher. Want to come over and try it out?"

I have a new library book I was planning to read this afternoon. The cover shows a girl in a shipwreck. But I can keep the book for three weeks. No need to finish it now.

"I'll be there in a few minutes."

I walk up the hill to our house. When I go into the kitchen, Mom has made *bao zi* to celebrate our spring break. While I eat one, I tell Mom how Ms. Simmons is getting married to a Mr. Sylvester this summer.

"How nice," Mom says. "We'll have to think of a wedding gift." Mom considers. "We could get her a good skillet."

Bao Zi

"I'm not sure if she likes to cook," I say.

"How about a picture frame?"

"I'm going down to Laura's," I say. "Can I take some *bao zi* over?"

"Does Laura like Chinese food?" Mom asks.

"I think she'd like to try it."

Mom puts the four nicest *bao zi* into a plastic container. I stuff it into my fabric lunch bag, and run out the door. The air smells damp, like spring.

When I get to the corner, I see Laura standing in her driveway, waiting for me.

"Hey, I brought you something," I say, catching my breath.

"What is it?"

"You'll see," I say, taking out the container and opening the lid.

Laura sniffs. "Smells good," she says. "What is it?"

"*Bao zi,*" I say. "A kind of bun with bean paste inside."

"*Bao zi,*" she repeats, trying to make the sounds right. She takes a bite. "I like it," she says. "Shee shee for the bowtsee."

"Hey, guess who our next year's teacher is," I say.

"Sylvester, whoever that is." Laura looks down.

"I know who it is," I say.

"You do?"

"Twenty questions."

"A lady?" Laura guesses.

"Yes," I answer.

"Does she teach at our school right now?"

"Yes."

"Fifth grade?"

"No."

"Do we know her?"

"Yes."

Laura sticks the rest of the *bao zi* in her mouth. "Do we know her well?"

I smile. "Very well."

"I give up."

"I'll give you a hint. She likes to ride bicycles."

Laura pulls her eyebrows together.

"And her mother's name is Olga."

"Ms. Simmons?!" Laura asks, grabbing my hand.

"She's getting married!" I say.

"To Mr. Sylvester!" Laura says.

"And I thought of a *great* wedding present," I say. "Mini cereal boxes!"

We go into Laura's house to get a piece of paper and some markers. Then we lie down on the floor to make a card for Mrs. Simmons. I fold the paper in half, and Laura writes *Congratulations* in fancy letters on the front.

"Do you know how to write that in Chinese?" she asks.

"My mom can show us." I say.

We decorate the inside of the card and then in big cursive letters, Laura writes *Love,* and we sign our names.